ONCE UPON
A
GOLDEN APPLE

WRITTEN BY JEAN LITTLE and MAGGIE DE VRIES
ILLUSTRATED BY PHOEBE GILMAN

VIKING

This book is dedicated to
Jonathan and Susanna, who started us off,
and to Mother Goose, the Brothers Grimm, Edward Lear,
L. Frank Baum, Lewis Carroll, Kenneth Grahame, Beatrix Potter,
Hans Christian Andersen, Iona and Peter Opie and Anonymous,
who helped us as we went along.
—J.L. and M. de V.

With love to Armand and Mark,
my brothers, my friends.
—P.G.

VIKING
Published by the Penguin Group
Penguin Books Canada Ltd, 10 Alcorn Avenue, Toronto, Ontario, Canada M4V 3B2
Penguin Books Ltd, 27 Wrights Lane, London W8 5TZ, England
Viking Penguin, a division of Penguin Books USA Inc.,
375 Hudson Street, New York, New York 10014, USA
Penguin Books Australia Ltd, Ringwood, Victoria, Australia
Penguin Books (NZ) Ltd, 182-190 Wairau Road, Auckland 10, New Zealand

Penguin Books Ltd, Registered Offices: Harmondsworth, Middlesex, England

First published 1991

3 5 7 9 10 8 6 4 2

Text Copyright © Jean Little and Maggie de Vries, 1991
Illustrations © Phoebe Gilman, 1991

*Publisher's note: This book is a work of fiction. Names, characters, places and inci-
dents either are the product of the author's imagination or are used fictitiously, and
any resemblance to actual persons living or dead, events, or locales is entirely
coincidental.*

Printed and bound in Italy on acid neutral paper.

Canadian Cataloguing in Publication Data
Little, Jean, 1932-
Once upon a golden apple

ISBN 0-670-82963-3

I. De Vries, Maggie.   II. Gilman, Phoebe, 1940-
III. Title.

PS8523.I87062 1990   jC813'.43   C90-093571-5
PZ7.L57On 1990

British Library Cataloguing in Publication Data Available
American Library of Congress Cataloguing in Publication Data Available

Once upon a . . .

golden apple . . .

Once upon a magic
pebble . . .

Once upon a singing
fiddle . . .

Once upon a time . . .

there lived Snow White and the three bears . . .

there lived Goldilocks and the seven dwarfs . . .

there lived Red Riding
Hood and Chicken
Little . . .

No! No!
No! No! No!

there lived a King and
Queen and their daughter,
Princess Briar Rose . . .

She kissed a cow with a crumpled horn . . .

She kissed a reluctant dragon . . .

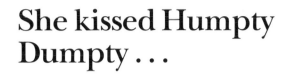

She kissed Humpty
Dumpty . . .

NO! NO! NO! NO! NO!

She kissed a frog . . . .

He turned into a
pumpkin . . .

He turned into a
gingerbread boy . . .

He turned into a roly-poly
pudding . . .

He turned into Prince
Valiant . . .

He looked at the Princess and said, "Off with her head!" …

He looked at her and said, "To market, to market, to buy a fat pig!" …

He looked at her and said, "I'll huff and I'll puff and I'll blow your house in!" . . .

He looked at her and said, "Shall we be married?". . .

They rode away on a little red hen . . .

They rowed away in a pea-green boat . . .

They rode away on a
spinning wheel . . .

They rode away on a milk-
white steed . . .

They rescued the Wicked Witch of the West . . .

They rescued the spider who sat down beside her . . .

They rescued three young rats in black felt hats . . .

They rescued Rock-a-Bye Baby . . .

They lived at the top of a beanstalk ...

They lived at the bottom of a well ...

They lived at the end of a
rainbow . . .

Well . . . maybe.

They all lived happily ever after.